Heetunka's Harvest

A TALE OF THE PLAINS INDIANS

Retold By Jennifer Berry Jones

Illustrated By Shannon Keegan

ROBERTS RINEHART PUBLISHERS
IN CONJUNCTION WITH
THE COUNCIL FOR INDIAN EDUCATION'S

For all the children of the Dakotas, especially Elise.

J.B.J.

For Dylan, Lauren, Blaine and Kyle.

S.K.

Acknowledgements:

Thanks to Wes, my husband, for his unflagging encouragement, patience, and invaluable advice. And special thanks to my friends and colleagues at Bismarck Public Library: Pamela A. Beaman, for assisting in my many interlibrary loan requests, and Marvia Boettcher, for cheering me on and on.

Text copyright © 1994 by Jennifer Berry Jones
Artwork copyright © 1994 by Shannon Keegan

Published in the United States of America by Roberts Rinehart Publishers
Post Office Box 666, Niwot, Colorado 80544

Published in Ireland and Great Britain by Roberts Rinehart Publishers
Main Street, Schull, West Cork, Republic of Ireland

International Standard Book Number 1-879373-17-3
Library of Congress Catalog Card Number 94-66093

Printed and Bound in Hong Kong by Colorcorp/Sing Cheong
Distributed in the United States and Canada by Publishers Group West

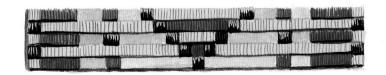

Heetunka, the Bean Mouse, dug up the last earth bean and tunneled through the dry prairie grass to the door of her underground storehouse. The light was fading from the autumn sky, and the nearly-bare branches of the river cottonwoods creaked in the wind.

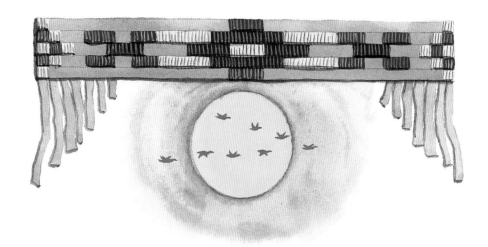

The small gray mouse was tired, but with this final trip, her pantry would be full. Her family could eat while the earth took its winter nap.

A chilly breeze ran along the ground, ruffling her thick fur, as Heetunka added the last bean to her shallow storehouse.

Soon, when the geese flew over a yellow moon, the women would come from their tipi encampment to trade with Heetunka, the Bean Mouse. They would come with quiet hearts and prayers of humble thanks for the seeds and rich white beans they would find in Heetunka's storehouse. And they would leave a fair trade for her.

To take such gifts without exchange would be wrong, for Heetunka always generously shared the food she had gathered for her own children.

And so each fall, the women came, just as their
grandmothers had come before them, bringing suet or
dried green corn in payment for Heetunka's harvest.
For each handful of beans they took, the women left
their thanks and their corn. With this trade, the
mouse-people shared the earth's fruits with their
Dakota sisters. So it had always been.

Above the prairie, an early-rising moon
hung low and yellow on the evening sky like a
rawhide drum. Over it passed a formation of geese,
southbound for the winter. Heetunka paused at the
door of her shallow nest and heard their distant calls.

Along the river, not far from Heetunka's nest,
a small winter camp was getting ready for the night.
Smoke from the tipi's cooking fires rose straight into
the cold night air.

As the geese flew high over the camp, the
sound of their honking reached a Dakota woman.
She paused in her cooking to listen. Lifting her face
towards the fading cries, she was reminded that

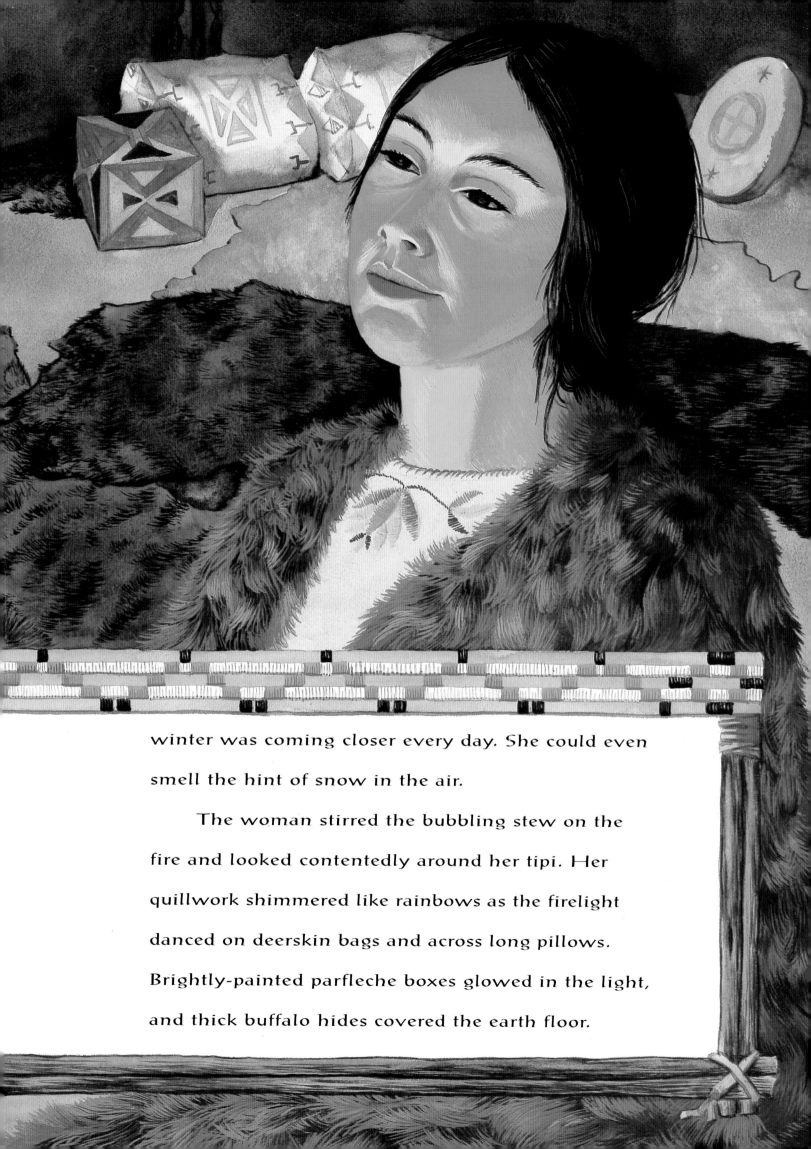

winter was coming closer every day. She could even

smell the hint of snow in the air.

The woman stirred the bubbling stew on the

fire and looked contentedly around her tipi. Her

quillwork shimmered like rainbows as the firelight

danced on deerskin bags and across long pillows.

Brightly-painted parfleche boxes glowed in the light,

and thick buffalo hides covered the earth floor.

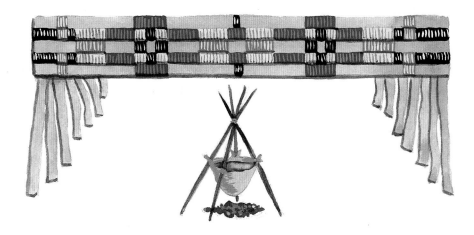

She was a good wife, she knew. Her family was well prepared for winter. Sage-smoked meats and pemmican cakes, her children's favorite, were safely packed in the rawhide boxes. Braided ropes of beaver grass were heavy with sliced and dried prairie turnips and squashes.

And a deerskin bag held plenty of good, green corn, traded from her Hidatsa neighbors. She had bartered well for it. Her softly-tanned buffalo hides had brought a good price.

Her family would fare well when the camp was snowbound and the buffalo vanished for days with the bitter weather. The woman smiled at her thriftiness.

As she cooked, she thought of one more thing: "Wouldn't some nice earth beans be fine in a stew! It's late in the season, so the mouse-people must be finished gathering their seeds. Tomorrow I'll search under the cottonwoods for their harvests."

Winter crept closer that night, spangling the willows with spikes of frost and edging the river with ice. The tipi smoke curled pink in the soft light of dawn as the woman and her family awoke.

The woman fed her family and then she took out a deerskin bag for the earth beans she knew she would find in Heetunka's storehouse.

But at the thought of the mouse's large pantry, the woman became greedy. She forgot her duty and the lessons she had learned from her grandmothers. Why should she share her fine corn with a mouse? Indeed, the words of her elders seemed silly to her now.

And so she took nothing to trade.

Near the river, the woman found Heetunka's narrow, crisscrossed trails in the matted grass. She followed them until they led her to a mouse-sized underground entrance. Then she took a stick and dug through the grasses and dirt which covered Heetunka's storehouse. But instead of offering a prayer of thanks, the selfish woman cried out, "Oh, little mouse, you've been busy. Look at the many, many beans you have gathered for me!"

Then the woman took them all: every bean Heetunka had worked so hard to gather.

Never pausing to offer thanks to her small sister of the woods, the woman thought only of the rich bean stew she would give to her family and the pride she would take from their smiles.

At twilight that evening, the woman was
gathering extra firewood by the river. She hummed to
herself, happy that because of her hard work, her
family was ready for the winter. Suddenly she thought
she heard crying. She stood perfectly still, and the
sound became louder.

"Who's that crying?" asked the woman.

"It's Heetunka, the Bean Mouse, crying for my
hungry children. Someone has taken all the food I
have worked so hard to gather. Oh, my poor little

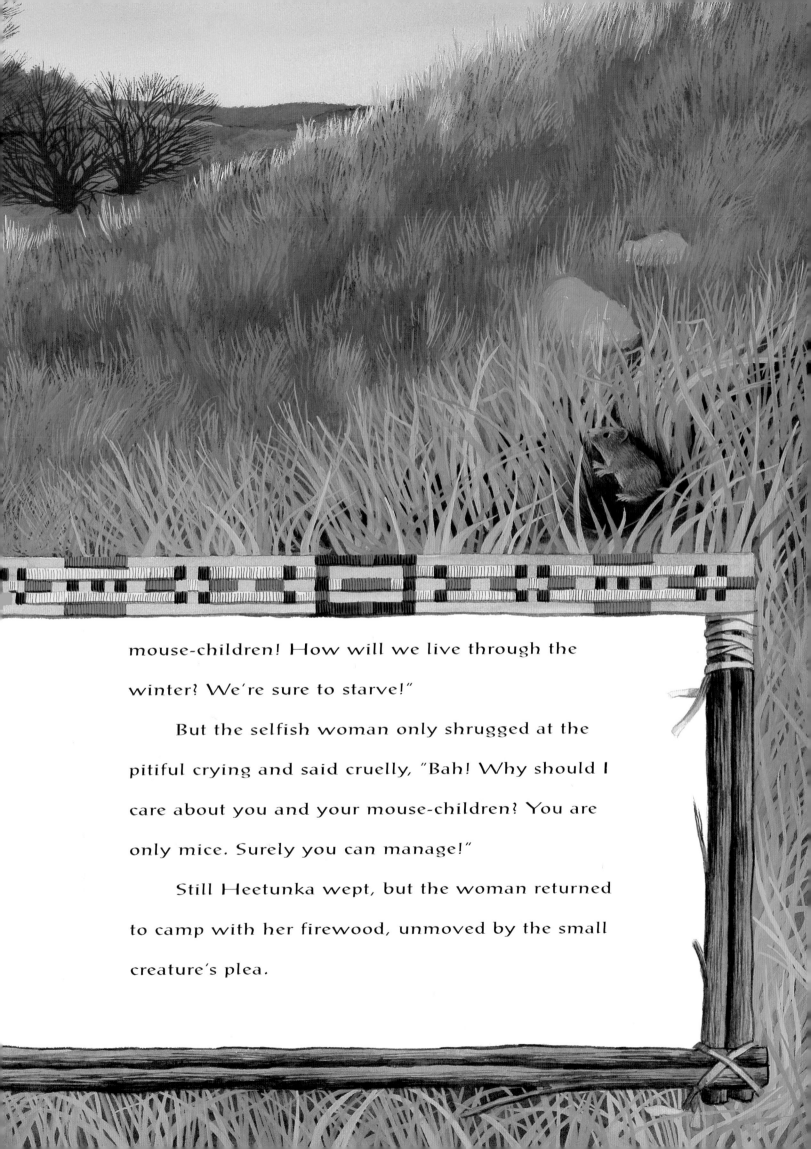

mouse-children! How will we live through the
winter? We're sure to starve!"

But the selfish woman only shrugged at the
pitiful crying and said cruelly, "Bah! Why should I
care about you and your mouse-children? You are
only mice. Surely you can manage!"

Still Heetunka wept, but the woman returned
to camp with her firewood, unmoved by the small
creature's plea.

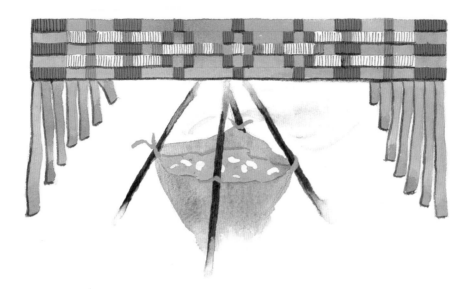

Smiling at her cleverness, the woman made dinner for her family, adding some of Heetunka's earth beans to the stew.

But that night, the woman tossed fitfully beneath her buffalo robe. Sleep teased her, but finally she dreamed that a spirit came to her. It was Hunka, the Spirit of Kinship, of Oneness-of-life, who said:

> YOU WERE WRONG TO TAKE ALL OF
>
> THE MOUSE-CHILDREN 'S FOOD.
>
> YOU MUST RETURN SOME BEANS,
>
> OR PUT CORN IN THEIR PLACE,
>
> OR YOUR OWN CHILDREN WILL HUNGER
>
> AND GO WITHOUT.

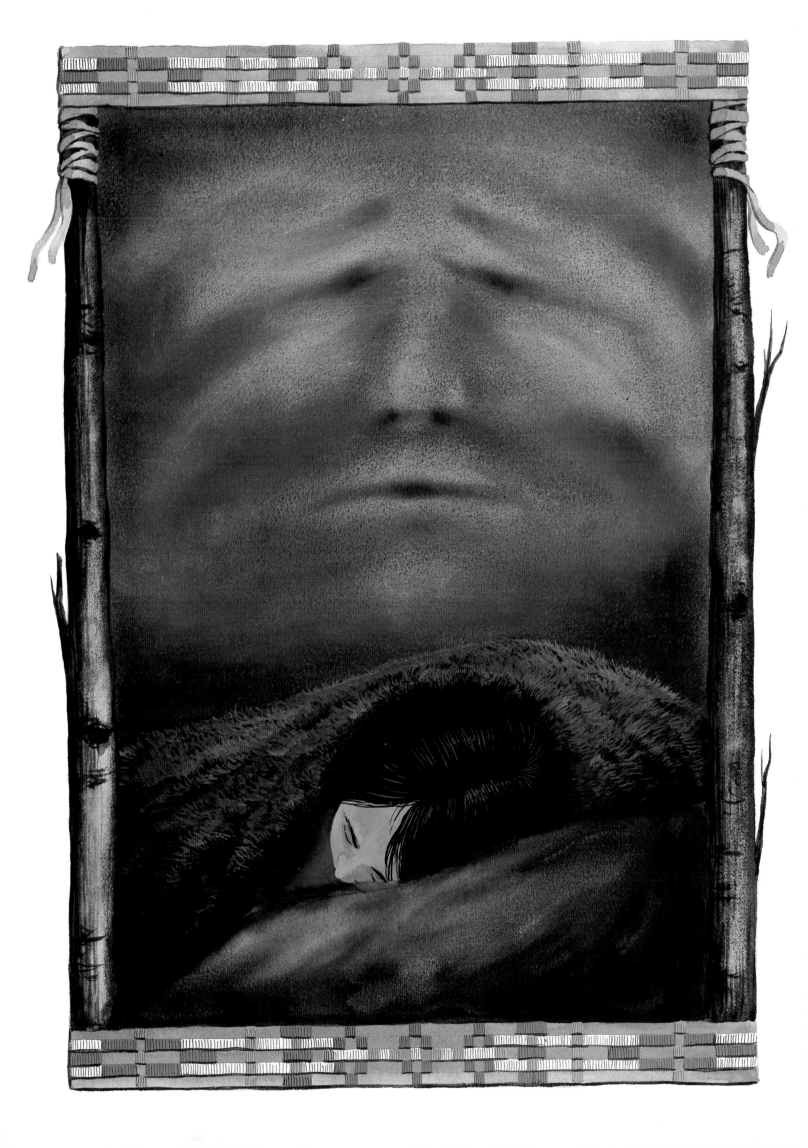

The woman woke with a start and shook her husband. "Husband! Wake up! I've just had the strangest dream!" And she told him about Hunka's visit to her.

"Wife," her husband said, after he had thought for a moment, "you'd better obey this vision. Hunka is warning you and will surely punish you if you don't do your duty."

"But I took beans from a lowly mouse," laughed the woman carelessly. "Why should I care about what those mice have for the winter?"

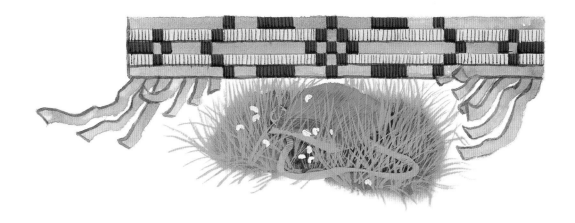

Her words had only just been spoken when the wind outside shifted, and a wave of thick gray smoke rolled over the bluff above the camp.

"Prairie fire!" cried the woman.

Like a hungry wolf, the fire leapt off the plains and down the steep bluffs, racing through the dry grasses around the camp and towards the woman's tipi.

The woman tried to gather up her boxes of food, her warm robes and embroidered pillows, but they were more than she could carry. Her husband pulled her by the arm as she snatched up the deerskin bag filled with Heetunka's beans.

"Hurry!" he cried, taking their children's hands.

The family fled their tipi and ran towards the river. In her haste, the woman tripped, scattering the beans deep into the tall grass, where the Bean Mouse would surely find them.

The woman and her family huddled by the river,
the children crying and afraid. As quickly as it had
come, the fire had vanished, leaving them staring at
the charred ruins of their home.

Their neighbors' tipis were untouched.

"My beautiful tipi," wailed the woman, "our

food, our clothing...all gone!"

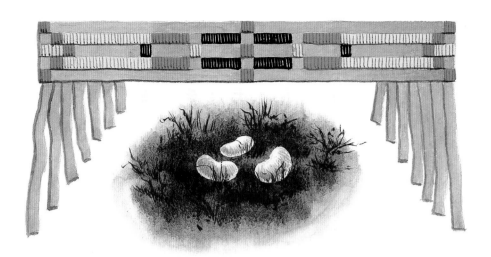

"You foolish woman," cried her husband, "Hunka has punished us all for your greediness. You stole from the Bean Mouse, and now look at what's happened! You don't deserve your husband, who provides you with so much. You don't even deserve your poor, helpless children."

"Husband, I am ashamed," said the woman, turning her back on the smoldering tipi and gathering her children to her. "In my rush to get ready for winter, I became selfish and ignored a simple duty. If only I had paid Heetunka! We had plenty of corn to share."

Her husband took pity on her. "My wife," he said, "it's true that now we'll be hard-pressed to make it through this winter. But some of our relatives are camped not far beyond the bend of the river. They'll take us in. Come, let's hurry before the snow starts."

The children, who had missed their breakfast, began to cry, but their mother said, "We'll eat soon, my little ones."

Then the family began their trek along the half-frozen river as the gentle snow began to fall.

HEETUNKA STILL GATHERS HER SEEDS

AND BEANS.

WHEN THE GEESE FLY SOUTH,

HER STOREHOUSE IS FULL.

SHE WILL HAPPILY SHARE WITH THOSE

WHO COME TO TRADE WITH HUMBLE,

THANKFUL HEARTS.

THE PAYMENT SHOULD BE GENEROUS:

GOOD GREEN CORN OR RICH SUET,

HANDFUL FOR HANDFUL OF BEANS REMOVED.

FOR ALTHOUGH HEETUNKA IS SMALL,

HER WORK IS BIG,

AND THOSE WHO WOULD GATHER

HER BEANS ARE INDEBTED TO HER,

FOR ALL NATURE IS ONE.

AUTHOR'S NOTE:

As early as October 11, 1804, the Bean Mouse was mentioned in the journal kept by Captain William Clark during his overland expedition of the American Northwest with Meriwether Lewis. Clark noted that he had eaten "a large Been...which is rich and verry nurrishing," taken from "the mice of the Prairie" by his Arikara hosts.

This retelling of the legend of the Bean Mouse is loosely modeled on the short version found in Melvin R. Gilmore's 1925 article, "The Ground Bean and its Uses" (*Indian Notes*, 2:178-187). I have not attempted to retell the story using the usual conventions of Native American oral tradition. Rather, it is my hope that details of daily Indian life in the days before European contact will add a new dimension to the legend for readers of all cultures.

The "Bean Mouse" is not a true mouse, but any of several species of voles (most probably *Microtus Pennsylvanicus*), which are widely distributed throughout North America. Larger than harvest mice, these particular voles are from 3-1/2 to 5 inches long, with chunky bodies, small ears, and a characteristic short tail. Their gray-brown fur is thick and soft. Voles typically gather large amounts of earth beans, seeds, and grains, which they store in shallow underground caches. The name "Heetunka" is a variation of the Siouan word for "mouse," which was used in a number of dialects to identify any species of mouse or vole.

The earth bean (*Ampicarpaea bracteata*) is also known as the ground bean or hog peanut, an annual vine bearing two kinds of fruit. The plant's small brown beans growing above ground are encased in pods; the underground fruits so prized by the Plains Indians and gathered by voles, are white, fleshy, and about the size of a lima bean.

GLOSSARY

Dakota: A large group of Siouan-speaking tribes of the North American Plains, commonly called Sioux, and living mostly in the Dakotas, northern Nebraska, and Minnesota.

Hidatsa: An American Indian group of North Dakota, the Hidatsa were agricultural peoples who traded corn, squash, and other vegetables with neighboring tribes, including the Sioux.

parfleche: Untanned hide (rawhide) soaked in lye and water to remove the hair and dried on a stretcher. Plains Indians made parfleche boxes and saddlebags.

pemmican: A food prepared by North American Indians from lean, sun-dried strips of meat pounded fine, mixed with fat (suet) and berries (choke-cherries), and pressed into small cakes.

quillwork: Porcupine quills, bleached, dyed, and intricately appliquéd to decorate hide, bark, or fabrics.

tipi: A cone-shaped tent of skins or bark, spread over a frame of poles, used by most of the North American Plains Indians.